SHOOT!

Crabtree Publishing Company
www.crabtreebooks.com

PMB 16A, 350 Fifth Avenue
Suite 3308
New York, NY 10118

612 Welland Avenue
St. Catharines, Ontario
Canada, L2M 5V6

Mayfield, Sue.
   Shoot! / Sue Mayfield ; illustrated by Ken Cox.
     p. cm. -- (Blue Bananas)
   Summary: Each member of Jamie Crocker's soccer team has a
special talent, but it takes their mascot, Shoot the dog, to help them
win the game.
     ISBN 0-7787-0847-0 -- ISBN 0-7787-0893-4 (pbk.)
    [1. Soccer--Fiction. 2. Dogs--Fiction.] I. Cox, Ken, 1973- . ill.
II. Title. III. Series.
PZ7.M4676 Sh 2002
[E]--dc21

                2001032436
                LC

Published by Crabtree Publishing in 2002
First published in 2000 by Mammoth
an imprint of Egmont Children's Books Limited
Text copyright © Sue Mayfield 2000
Illustrations © Ken Cox 2000
The Author and Illustrator have asserted their moral rights.
Paperback ISBN 0-7787-0893-4
Reinforced Hardcover Binding ISBN 0-7787-0847-0

SHOOT!

SUE MAYFIELD
ILLUSTRATED BY KEN COX

Blue Bananas

For my own dog Moss
who also loves soccer
S.M.

To Margot and Sam
K.C.

Hi! I'm Jamie. Jamie Crocker.

Jamie Crocker, mad about soccer!

Jamie's my name, and soccer's my game!

I play with my friends.

We're a team. We're the dream team!

We are J.C. UNITED!

Let me introduce the team:

I'm the captain, J.C.

(That's Jamie Crocker,

mad about soccer!)

I play in the center.

I dodge and kick.

I turn and flick.

Watch
this kick,

Then there's Darren Paul.

Darren Paul, best with the ball!

He's sharp and he's fast – light on his toes.

He can balance the ball on his nose!

This is Maxine Cole.

She plays in goal.

Maxine Cole – great in goal!

She stretches and saves.

A punch and a dive.

What a save, Maxine!

Give me five!

This is Simon Shredders.

Simon Shredders – wicked at headers!

Watch him jump, reaching tall.

Simon Shredders heads the ball!

Easy!

And this is William Storer.

William Storer!

What a scorer!

William shoots and you can bet

He puts the ball right in the net!

So that's the team. J.C. United.

And I must not forget . . .

This is Maxine Cole's dog, Shoot!

Shoot plays soccer too.

Shoot is just like one of the team.

Shoot dribbles

Shoot scores

With his nose

And with his paws!

He does headers

He does kicks

High tackles

Tail flicks!

When we train, Shoot trains.

When we take a break,

Shoot takes one too.

Last Saturday we had a match against Ricky's Rockets. It was a five-a-side match. It was on a field in the park.

J.C. United is the best.

Put tho
Rockets
the tes

Mom and Dad came to watch. So did Maxine's grandpa. Maxine's grandpa brought Shoot to watch too.

William's grandma knitted hats and scarves for everyone. They were blue and white – the same as our shirts. Maxine tied a scarf around Shoot's neck.

Ricky's Rockets had yellow shirts. Their
captain had no front teeth. Their goalie
was HUGE!

"Come on, Rockets!" shouted their moms
and dads.

GRRR!

We jogged onto the field.

I did some juggling

with the ball.

Mom and Dad and

Maxine's grandpa started to shout.

"J.C. United – the whites and blues.

J.C. United never lose!"

"We'll see about that," said one

of the Rockets, picking his nose.

Maxine ran to her net and

did some stretching exercises. She put

on her special goalkeeper gloves.

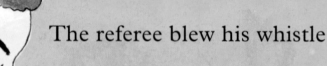

The referee blew his whistle and we were off.

I got the ball and passed it to Darren Paul.

Darren ran down the field.

He kicked it to William. William dodged past the Rockets' captain.

He kicked high to Simon . . .

And Simon Shredders scored with a
header. We all ran and hugged him
and shouted, "Simon Shredders, Simon
Shredders, Simon Shredders is wicked
at headers!"

That was one-nothing for us.

Aaargh!

Then Ricky's Rockets got the ball.

A boy with red hair ran down

the wing. William tackled him.

William got the ball. He passed

it to Darren Paul.

Darren Paul!
Darren Paul!

Darren dribbled it. Darren ran down the field. Darren shot at the goal . . . Darren scored! HURRAY! Two-nothing. We patted him on the back.

The Rockets' moms and dads started to shout. "Rock-ets! Rock-ets! Rock-ets! ROCK-ETS!" Louder and louder they shouted. The Rockets took a throw-in. A tall thin boy did a header. Then their captain got the ball and ran for the goal.

Come on, Rockets! It's blast-off time.

"Pass! Pass!" said the boy with the red hair. But the captain kept running. He took a shot at the goal. The ball soared through the air. Maxine jumped. She punched the ball. She knocked it over the bar. What a save!

No Sweat!

Maxine took a goal kick.

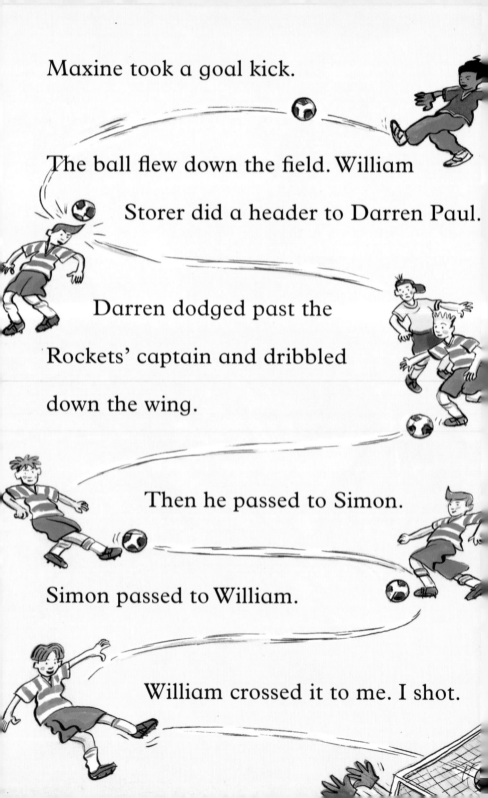

The ball flew down the field. William

Storer did a header to Darren Paul.

Darren dodged past the

Rockets' captain and dribbled

down the wing.

Then he passed to Simon.

Simon passed to William.

William crossed it to me. I shot.

I scored!

That made it three-nothing.

We were well ahead.

The referee blew his whistle for halftime.

We ran to the side of the field. Simon

Shredders' dad arrived on his bike.

He gave us oranges to suck.

Great play, United. Keep it up.

In the second half everything went wrong. As soon as the referee blew his whistle the red-haired boy got the ball. He ran down the wing and scored over Maxine's head.

That made it three-one.

The Rockets were cheering and clapping and chanting. Then their captain got the ball. William Storer tackled him but he kept running. Darren Paul tackled him but he kept running. Darren slipped and fell over.

The Rockets scored again in the corner of the net. Maxine dived to save it, but it was out of reach.

Now it was three-two. We still had a lead but not by much. Maxine was frowning.

Simon Shredders got the ball.

He kicked it to William.

William ran in to shoot

but then his shoe flew off.

By the time he'd put it

on again the tall thin

boy had the ball.

He was running

towards the goal.

He kicked it.

Maxine saved it.

We cheered.

But then he kicked

again . . . and scored.

Oh no! My shoe!

It was three-three with just five minutes to go. We didn't want to tie. We wanted to win. We needed another goal and we needed it fast.

"COME ON, UNITED!" yelled Dad.

We've got to make a comeback.

They'll never stop us now.

William passed the ball to me. I passed it to Simon. Simon kicked it to Darren. Then the Rockets tackled. Darren fell to the ground. The referee blew his whistle. "Foul!" said the referee. He gave a free kick to Simon Shredders. But Darren was hurt. His leg was sore. A first aid woman ran onto the field and helped him off. Everybody cheered for him.

Oh no! Now we only had four players!

Ricky's Rockets had five. They had the

ball too. They ran, they passed, they

shot at the goal . . . but Maxine saved it.

Maxine smiled and punched the air.

Maxine threw the ball to William.

William dribbled down the center.

He passed it to me. I dodged past

the Rockets' defense. I passed to Simon.

Simon was ready to score.

"Shoot!" Maxine cried.

In the crowd, Shoot heard his name.

Quick as a flash . . .

He slipped his leash.

He jumped the fence.

He bounded onto the field.

Shoot ran past the Rockets' defense.

He ran towards the net.

Shoot's scarf was flapping behind him.

Hey! No dogs allowed.

The referee blew his whistle.

"Stop!" he said. "There's a dog on the field."

"He's a member of the team," said Maxine's grandpa.

"He's wearing blue and white," said my mom.

"He's our substitute!" I said suddenly.

The referee shook his head.

"Play on," he said.

It was still three-three.

Simon had the ball.

The Rockets tackled him.

He passed it to me.

I passed it to William.

William ran . . .

crossed it to me . . .

I crossed it to Shoot . . .

and Shoot . . .

headed it into the net with his nose!

"GOAL!" I shouted.
Goal for the dog!
Goal for Shoot!
Scores for our team!
Scores with his snoot!
That's it. The end
of the game.
We had won.

J.C. United had won. We jumped in the air.

Shoot jumped in the air too!

Maxine put her arms round him and
hugged him. Shoot licked her nose.

Then he barked and wagged his tail.

We won a trophy.

Mom filled it with lemonade.

Simon's dad took a photograph.

Then we rode home in Maxine's grandpa's van. We were all singing,

"J.C. United, we are the best!

We are better than all the rest!

J.C. United better by far . . .

But Shoot is the hero!

Shoot is the star!"

BLue Bananas

Don't forget there's a whole bunch of Blue Bananas to choose from: